This book belongs to

_____

For the bairns: Rio, Skye, Aura, Sophia and Izzy

Picture Kelpies is an imprint of Floris Books
First published in 2012 by Floris Books Second printing 2012
Text © 2012 Gill Arbuthnott Illustrations © 2012 Joanne Nethercott
Gill Arbuthnott and Joanne Nethercott assert their right under the Copyright, Designs and
Patents Act 1988 to be recognised as the Author and Illustrator of this Work.
All rights reserved. No part of this book may be reproduced without prior permission of
Floris Books, 15 Harrison Gardens, Edinburgh www.florisbooks.co.uk
The publisher acknowledges subsidy from Creative Scotland towards the
publication of this volume. British Library CIP Data available
ISBN 978-086315-870-4
Printed in Poland

Lost at the Zoo

Gill Arbuthnott
and Joanne Nethercott

Rory the mouse was excited. He often went out for trips in Sam's pocket, but he'd never been to the zoo before.

His whiskers twitched and he sniffled and snuffled as he poked his head out and breathed deeply.
There were so many smells it made him dizzy. Some were delicious, some were delightful and some were downright disgusting.

From the top of the hill, Rory felt as though he could see the whole world. The wind whizzed through his whiskers and made his ears flap.

"Make sure you stay in my pocket," said Sam. "You wouldn't like being lost here."

Anteaters

Zebras

Lions

Owls

Rhinos

Flamingos

Penguins

Koalas

The sign on the first building said ANTEATER but all Rory could see was a swishing tail. He leaned out of Sam's pocket to get a better look.

He leaned further...

and further...

Squee

...eeeak!

Rory lost his grip and
fell – into the enclosure.

"Help!" squeaked Rory.
But Sam didn't hear him.

Rory felt a gust of hot breath on his neck.
He looked up...

A small pair of eyes on a long, long nose peered back.

"What's wrong?" asked the anteater.

"I've lost Sam," Rory said.

"Dearie me! What does Sam look like?"

"He's got a stripy coat," said Rory.

"Och, then he's just over there."

The anteater pointed with his huge claws.
Rory scampered through a fence onto a
grassy hillside. He could see something
stripy.
But it wasn't Sam. It was...

...a ZEBRA.

"Good morning," the zebra said politely. "Can I help you?"

"I've lost Sam," said Rory.

"Well, what does he look like?"

"He's got sticky-out sandy hair," said Rory.

"Oh, I know where Sam is." The zebra tossed
her black-and-white mane. "Try next door."

Rory darted over and squeezed under the fence.
He was whisker to whisker with something that had sticky-out
sandy hair. But it wasn't Sam. It was...

...a LION.
The lion yawned.
Rory gulped.
"Yes?" it growled
grumpily. "You woke
me up."
"S-s-sorry," squeaked
Rory. "I was looking for
Sam, but he's not
here."
"Clearly not," said
the lion, flexing
his claws. "Does
Sam look like me?"

RC

"N-n-no," stuttered Rory. "He's a lot smaller, and he's got big round eyes." "Go away then. Try that tall tree down the hill." The lion let out an angry

OOAAAR!

Squeeeak!

Rory raced down the hill. Two big round eyes blinked at him from high in a tree. But it wasn't Sam. It was...

...an OWL.

"Whooo whooo Whooo are yooou?"

asked the owl.
"Have yooou come to stay?"

"Er... no," said Rory. "I'm looking for Sam."

"I don't know Sam, but I think yooou'd like it here.
I'm very fond of mice."

That's kind, thought Rory.

He looked round the owl's home.

There were trees and bushes.

A nice neat nest box.

And a little pile of white bones, just the right size for...

...MOUSE BONES! Squeeeak!

Rory ran for it, just as the owl swooped down.

Rory hid behind a big grey boulder. His heart was pitter-pattering. Which way now?

He sniffled and snuffled, but he couldn't smell Sam.

He scrambled and clambered up the boulder.

He stared and searched,
but he couldn't see Sam.

Suddenly, Rory
tumbled off, as the
boulder stood up,
and...

...Rory was nose to
horn with a RHINO.

"Hello," it said. "You're very wee. Who are you?"
"I'm Rory, and I'm trying to find Sam."
"What does Sam look like? Is he as big as me?"
"No, but he's got long legs."
The rhino pointed with his huge horn. "Try over there, wee Rory."

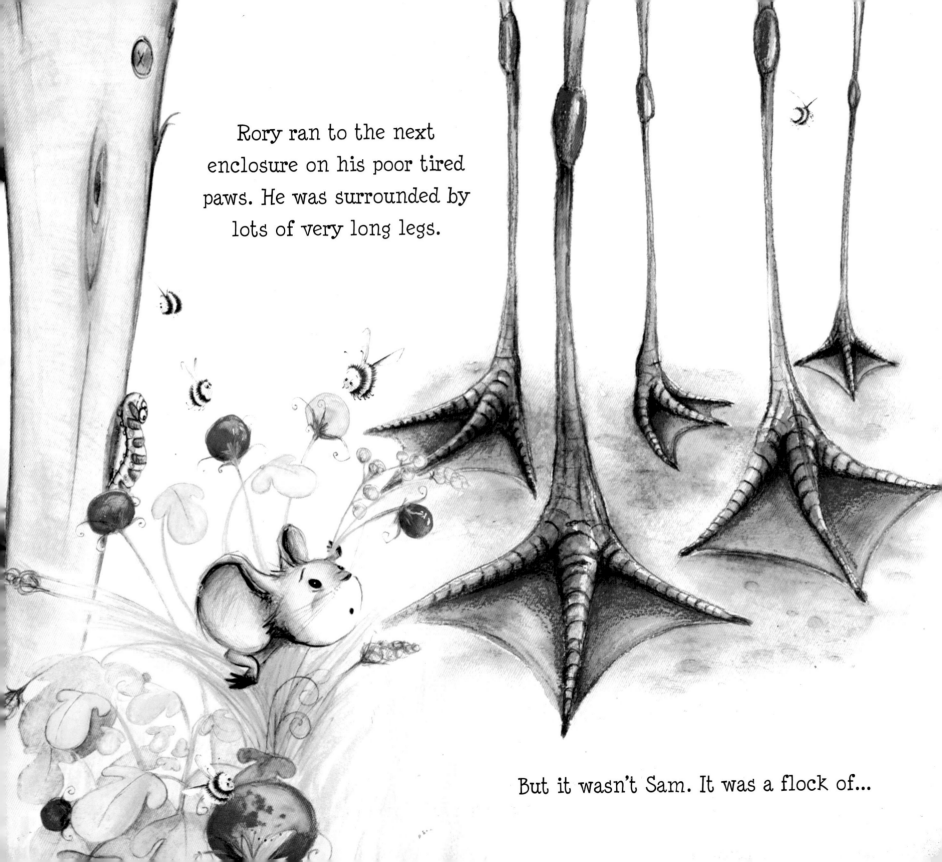

Rory ran to the next enclosure on his poor tired paws. He was surrounded by lots of very long legs.

But it wasn't Sam. It was a flock of...

...FLAMINGOS.

"I'll never find Sam!" Rory squeaked.
"Is there a problem?" asked a
friendly flamingo, twisting her
graceful, pink neck to look at him.
  "I've lost Sam and I don't think I'll
ever find him."
"I've never heard of a Sam. You
should ask the penguins, over there."

She pointed with her wide, curved beak.
"They're terrible blethers, but they
know everything."

  'Thank you," said Rory,
and he crept wearily off.

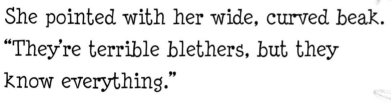

The penguins were arguing. The noise was terrible and the smell of fish was even worse. Rory didn't know whether to put his paws over his ears or his nose.

"Excuse me," he said.

"EXCUSE ME," he said more loudly.

"EXCUSE ME!" he yelled.

The penguins stopped squabbling and turned to look at Rory.

"Yes?" they chorused.

"I'm Rory and I've lost Sam. The flamingo said you might know where he is."

"He might be at the pandas," said the first penguin.

"Och no, Peg. He'll likely be at the eagles."

"What about the chimps, Jeannie?"

"Or the gibbons, Maggie?"

Soon all the penguins were arguing again and there
were flippers and beaks pointing everywhere.

"Quiet everyone!" Peg yelled at the others.
"We're away for a walk, Rory, and a wee bite to eat.
Come with us and tell us what Sam looks like."
Rory scurried along beside the penguins.
"Sam's got a stripy coat, and sticky-out sandy
hair, and big round eyes, and long legs, and I'm
afraid I'm never going to find him."

"THERE HE IS!"

shouted all the penguins.
Rory looked round...

It was SAM!

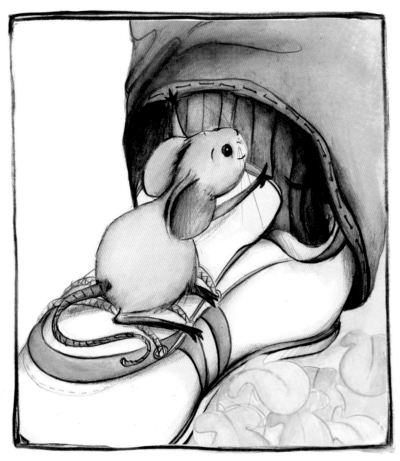

Rory thanked the penguins for their help.
Then he scampered across to Sam, scrambled
onto his shoe and scratched his ankle.

"What are you doing down there, Rory?" Sam said, picking him up. "I told you to stay in my pocket. Imagine if you'd got lost out there with all these animals!"

Just imagine, thought Rory, as he snuggled down in Sam's pocket, safe at last.

The tail end.

The **BIG** BOTTOM HUNT

Lari Don
Illustrated by
Gabby Grant

How to Make a Heron Happy

Lari Don
and Nicola O'Byrne

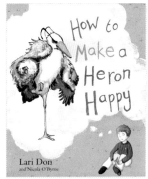

Orange Juice Peas!

Lari Don
and Lizzie Wells

Wee Granny's MAGIC BAG

Elizabeth McKay   Maria Bogade

My Cat Mac

Margaret Forrester and Sandra Klaassen

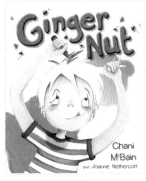

Ginger Nut

Chani McBain
and Joanne Nethercott

Lewis Clowns Around

Lynne Rickards
and
Gabby Grant

Fergus finds a Friend

Kenneth Steven
Illustrated by Louise Crosby

Bagpipes Beasties and Bogles

Tim Archbold

Uan the Little Lamb

'A delight'
Books for Keeps

Sandra Klaassen

HUNGRY HETTIE
The Highland Cow who won't stop eating!

Illustrated by
JO ALLAN

HAIRY HETTIE
The Highland Cow who needs a haircut!

Illustrated by
JO ALLAN

Original Scottish picture books to enjoy together

 Scan me!

Thistle Street
A braw Scots story for bairns
MIKE NICHOLSON AND CLAIRE KEAY

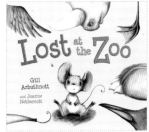

Lost at the Zoo

Gill Arbuthnott
and Joanne Nethercott

YOU CAN'T PLAY HERE!

Angus Corby

picturekelpies.co.uk   Find Picture Kelpies on